In My Mother's House

In My Mother's House

By Ann Nolan Clark

ILLUSTRATED BY VELINO HERRERA

PUFFIN BOOKS

PUFFIN BOOKS

Published by the Penguin Group

Viking Penguin, a division of Penguin Books USA Inc.,

375 Hudson Street, New York, New York 10014, U.S.A.

Penguin Books Ltd, 27 Wrights Lane, London W8 5TZ, England

Penguin Books Australia Ltd, Ringwood, Victoria, Australia

Penguin Books Canada Ltd, 10 Alcorn Avenue, Toronto, Ontario, Canada M4V 3B2

Penguin Books (N.Z.) Ltd, 182–190 Wairau Road, Auckland 10, New Zealand

Penguin Books Ltd, Registered Offices: Harmondsworth, Middlesex, England

First published in the United States of America by The Viking Press, 1941
Reissued in 1991
Published in Puffin Books, 1992

3   5   7   9   10   8   6   4   2

Copyright Ann Nolan Clark, 1941
Copyright renewed Ann Nolan Clark, 1969
All rights reserved

LIBRARY OF CONGRESS CATALOGING-IN-PUBLICATION DATA
Clark, Ann Nolan, 1898–
In my mother's house / by Ann Nolan Clark ; illustrated by Velino
Herrera.   p.   cm.
Originally published: New York : Viking Press, 1941.
Summary: A young Tewa Indian describes the homes, customs, work,
and strong communal spirit of his people.
ISBN 0-14-054496-8 (pbk.)
1. Tewa Indians—Juvenile poetry.   2. Children's poetry, American.
[1. Tewa Indians—Poetry.   2. Indians of North America—Poetry.
3. American poetry.]   I. Herrera, Velino, ill.   II. Title.
[PS3505.L228I5   1992]   811'.52—dc20   91-30185

Printed in the United States of America
Set in Garamond #3

Contents

HOME

This is my Mother's house;
My Father made it.
He made it with adobe bricks;
He made it strong;

He made it big;
He made it high;
My Mother's house,
I live in it.

6

This is my Mother's house;
My Mother plastered it
With brown clay;
On the outside
My Mother plastered it.

The inside walls are white;
My Mother made them white;
The floor is smooth;
My Mother made it smooth,
For me to live there.

7

In my Mother's house
There is a fireplace:
The fireplace holds the fire.
On dark nights the fire is bright;
On cold nights the fire is warm.
The fire is always there,
To help me see,
To keep me warm.

In my Mother's house
There are the grinding stones:
The big, flat holding stone,
The small rubbing stone;
The grinding stones,
My Mother's grinding stones.

On the floor
Beside her stones
My Mother kneels,
And with her hands
She grinds the corn;
Yellow corn and blue corn
My Mother grinds
For me to eat.

8

Red chili and meat and melons
And yellow cornmeal
I have to eat.

Apricots and peaches
And little red plums
I have to eat.

Big round tortillas
And brown frijoles
I have to eat.
I eat them;
I like them.

In my Mother's house
All day
I play and work;
All night
I sleep.

The walls come close around me
In a good way.

I can see them;
I can feel them;
I live with them.

This house is good to me,
It keeps me;
I like it,
My Mother's house.

My Mother's house,
It does not stand alone.
Its sister houses are around it;
Its sister houses are close to it.

Like holding hands,
The houses stand close together
Around the plaza.

Houses are the stay-in places, THE PUEBLO
But the plaza
Is the live-in place
For all the people.

In the plaza the people work;
In the plaza the people play
And sing and dance
And make ready for feasting.
It is the place
For all the people.

The plaza keeps the people together,
And the houses
With their backs to the mountains,
Stand facing the plaza
And shut it in.

My Mother's house,
It does not stand alone;
Its sister houses
Are all around it.

THE PEOPLE

We are the people
Living together,
All of us together.

We live here
In the houses,
In the plaza
Together.

When it is dark
All of us are sleeping.

When it is day
We are working,

Always
Together.

It is good to stand close
Like our houses.

The Wise Ones
Are our Fathers.
They tell us what to do;
They keep us;

Like the plaza,
They keep us
Together.

THE COUNCIL

15

FIELDS   Brown fields,
With ground all broken,
I walk softly over you.
I would not hurt you,
While you keep
The baby corn seeds sleeping.

See, brown fields,
The sun will shine for you;
The sun will warm you,
And make you happy.

16

Soon the rains will come
And wet you,
And give you water
For your baby corn seeds sleeping.
The sun will call the corn seeds;
The rain will call the corn seeds;
They will push up;
Little corn seeds will push up,
Up through the broken ground,
Little corn seeds growing.

Brown fields,
You will turn to green;
Little green corn ears
Growing,

Little green corn ears
Dancing,
For the rain,
For the sun.

Time to gather them,
Blue corn and red corn;
Time to harvest them,
Yellow corn and white corn.

There will be dancing;
There will be feasting,
Thanking the sun and the rain
For corn.

Then, brown fields,
Hide away in your blanket,
In your snow blanket.
Sleep, if you want to,
My Father will call you,
When it is time again,
Time again for the corn.

We could have more fields
If the little hills
Did not come down
To the fences
That our Fathers made.
We could have more fields
If the little river
Were bigger
And had more water
To give the thirsty crops.

ARROYOS We could have more fields,
If the arroyos
Did not come creeping,
Creeping,
Under the fences,
Under all the fences,

Creeping,
Creeping,
Eating away
Our Father's land.

We watch arroyos grow,
Like a bad thing,
Getting deeper,
Getting wider,
Creeping
Under the fences,
Eating the land.

One thing we know,
Though we are little.
We know that arroyos are bad;
We know that we must stop them
Before they eat
All of our Father's land.

PASTURE Beyond my Father's fields,
Beyond the little river,
Up
And down
And all around
The little hills,
Is pasture
For the people's horses.

This land was made
That grass might grow upon it,
Thick growing grass,
Strong growing grass,
Sweet growing grass
For our horses to feed on,
For our cows to feed on,
Grazing.

22

Indians must keep their land.
They must keep the land they have;
They must not sell it;

They must not let other people   LAND
Take it.

Indians must keep
What land they have.

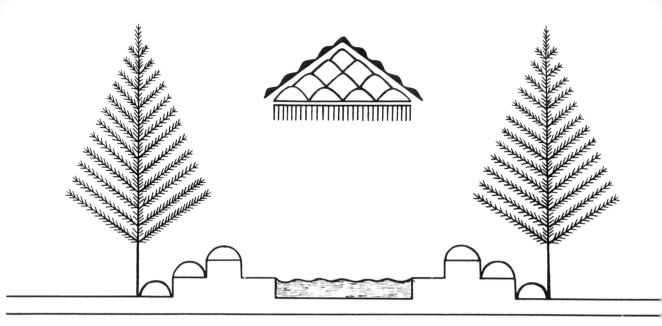

Lakes
Are the holding-places
For water,
As the fireplace
Is the holding-place
For fire,
As the plaza
Is the holding-place
For people.

But
My heart is the holding-place,
My heart is the keeping-place
For the things I know
About that lake in the mountains.
Always will I keep
In my heart

I know a lake in the mountains;
My Grandfather told me about it,
My Father told me,
My Mother's Brother told me;

The things that belong there,
As lakes
Keep water
For the people.

24

Up in the high places
Rivers are little;
I can step over them,
They are so little.

Little rivers
Bring their waters
To bigger rivers.

The biggest river
Is the Rio Grande;
It takes the water
From the little rivers
And keeps it
For its own.

Our Fathers
Made the ditches
To carry the water
To the fields.

The biggest ditch
Is Mother Ditch,
Acequia Madre.

The little ones
Are the feeder ditches;
They are the helpers
For Acequia Madre.

In the spring
Before it is time
For planting,
Our Fathers clean the ditches
And make them ready
To receive new waters.
And our Mothers
Come walking

All the way from their houses
With lunches
In their shawls
And in their hands
And on their heads
For our Fathers to eat,
While they are cleaning the
    ditches.

26

IRRIGATION When my Father
Needs water
For his thirsty fields,
He opens the ditches
To let the water run slowly,
Slowly,
Around the roots
Of all the growing things.

My Father
Closes the ditches
To stop the water,
When his fields
Have finished drinking.

28

My Father
Opens the ditches
When it is his day
To irrigate his fields.

No one
Would take a day
That was not his
To irrigate.

No one
Would take too much water

When it was his day
To irrigate.

All Indians
Are taught,
When they are little,
That water is good;
It must not be wasted.

I have known this
For a long time.

THE WINDMILL

A windmill is high,
A windmill is round,
A windmill is almost cloud color.

A windmill sings
When the wind is little,
But sometimes at night
I hear the windmill crying.

Today I am laughing
At the windmill;
It goes round and round,
And round
And round,
Like Zuni man
Dancing
Comanche Dance.

Last year,
When we were small,
There was a spring
Near the river.

It made the grass green
That grew around it.
But the water
Of that spring
Kept running,
Running.

It turned the land
Into a swamp;
It was not good.

Cows and horses went there
To eat the green grass;
They could not go away again,
Because the swamp
Held them.

Then
Our Fathers
Worked together;
They made a pipeline
And piped the water
From the spring
To a tank.

Pipes bring water
From the spring
To store it
In the storage tank.

Pipes take water
From the storage tank
To the pueblo,
To bring water
To our houses
In the pueblo.

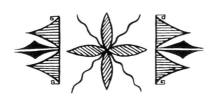

31

Now
The land around the spring
Is not a swamp,
To hold the cows and horses
When they are looking
For green grass.

It is good land now,
Because the water in the spring
Is working,

Working,
Not just running,
Running.

And we have water
In our houses
To help
Our Mothers
Keep us clean.

Cows just stand
Eating
And looking
And eating,
Always eating.

Sometimes I go after the cows;
On my horse
I go after the cows
And bring them home.

Some cows   cows
Give us milk
To drink;
And some cows
My Father shoots
With a gun,
And my Mother
Cuts the meat
In little pieces
And hangs it to dry
In the sun,
To get it ready
For me to eat.

SHEEP I have seen sheep
Walking slowly,
Their little feet
Making deep holes
In the ground.

This I know:
I know
That sheep give their wool
To people
To weave into cloth
For blankets and for coats.

We do this a little
But not much.
We kill our sheep
To eat.

I have seen goats   GOATS
Climb high rocks
And jump down again,
As if they were playing.

34

This is my horse.
His mane is dark cloud,
His tail is dark cloud.

Like the wind
He goes swiftly;
Like the lightning
He goes swiftly.

We go together,
My horse and I;
We go together,
Swiftly, together.

It is good
To have horses,
Many horses.

35

In the fields
We use our horses
For planting.
In the threshing ring
The horses go round and round
And thresh the wheat.

Our horses bring the wagons,
Loaded with corn,
From the fields to the plaza.
Our horses carry us swiftly
Over the mountains
To hunt the deer.

It is good to have horses, many horses.

TREES   Trees are good to us;
They give us things,
Many things.

Trees give us
Shade
From sun;
They give us
Shelter
From storm.

Trees give us
Fruits and nuts,

Apricots,
Little and yellow,
And plums and apples.

Trees give us
Brown little piñon nuts
Hiding away
In their pine cones.

They give us wood
For our houses,
And wood to burn
In the fireplace.

38

In the high mountains
We go for aspen,
Tall, straight aspen,
White, slender aspen,
To make the vigas
For our houses.

On the fat mountain sides,
Not high up,
We go for piñon
And cedar boughs.

We pack them on our backs
To our houses
Below,
By the river.

Piñon and cedar boughs
We bring home
For firewood.

Crackling cedar,
Sweet smelling piñon
We bring home
To burn.

Wild plants
Give their seeds
To the wind
To scatter them,
Not just in fields
But everywhere.

JUNIPER

Juniper,
Juniper berries,
So blue,
So pretty.

Wild plants
Grow on hills
And by the roads,
Outside of fences,
Along the ditches,
Everywhere.

You make medicine
To make me well;
You make hair wash
To make my hair shine,
Little juniper berries.

Wild plants have flowers;
They dance with butterflies
And with me too,
When I sing to them.

You make dye,
Black dye
And brown dye
And sometimes green dye,
Little blue juniper berries.

Wild plants
Are friends to us;
They give us things.

INDIAN TEA

Indian tea
Is a little flower;
It looks like a tall girl,
Standing in the high grass.

It looks like an Indian girl
Waiting for someone;
Swaying to listen
For someone coming.

44

My Mother
Does not think that.
She thinks that Indian tea
Is good to drink
And good to use as medicine.

She thinks that Indian tea
Is good to use for colors;
It can make her wool yarn
Green,
And yellow like the sun,

And another yellow
Like new flowers.

But I like best to think
Of Indian tea
As a tall girl waiting;
An Indian girl waiting,
Standing in the tall grass
And swaying to listen
For the footsteps of someone.

YUCCA

Yucca
Growing
So tall,
Like candles;
So white,
Like candles;
With a flower
For light.

We twist your little leaves
Into strings of thread;

We knot your strong stems
Into rope.
We weave your fibers
Into mats and baskets;
We pound your roots
For soap to make us clean.

Yucca,
Tall, white Yucca,
You make my heart sing
With your beauty.

46

Chamiso
Grows thick and high
By the side of the road
And the arroyos.

In the summer
It wears new green,
But in autumn,
When the corn is ripe,
Chamiso wears yellow flowers.
Yellow,
Yellow,
Chamiso wears yellow flowers
      in autumn.

Chamiso
Gives us colors
For blankets,
If we want them;
Yellow dye,
And green dye,
If we want them.

When we are sick,
Chamiso gives us medicine
To drink
To make us well.

GUACO

In the spring
Guaco is new green
And little.

If we pick it then
Our Mothers will cook it,
With the chili
And the beans.

In the summer
Guaco grows tall,
Taller than I
And taller than my Brother.

It has purple flowers in summer.
They bend down to look at us.

In autumn
The guaco flowers go away
And in their places
Come the seed pods,
The long, green seed pods,
Holding the seeds,
The baby seeds
Of guaco,
For a new year.

48

Our Mothers
Dry guaco flowers,
And the leaves and stems.
They grind them into flour
To mix with cornmeal
To make us bread.

Our Mothers gather
The flowers of guaco,
And the leaves and stems;
They boil them together
On a fire in the plaza;

For many days
They boil the guaco.

They make little, soft cakes
Of the boiled-down guaco,
And wrap them
In corn-husk blankets
To dry into paint,
Into black paint,
To make the designs
On pottery.

I know the tracks
Of bear
And deer
And mountain lion.

I know the marks
The rabbit makes,
And the foot-prints
Of the coyote.

I know where the beavers
Build their houses
Across the river.

I know where the prairie-dogs
Have little towns
In the tall grasses.

I know
How to call wild turkey,
Eating red berries
On the mountain side.

I know
What the owl says;
When it is dark,
I do not like it.

I know
Where the eagle nests
With its babies
On the sides of high rocks.

I know
These things;
My Father told me.

MOUNTAINS Mountains are the high places;
They reach up and up
To the blue-blue above.

They stand around us,
Looking down at the people
In the pueblo,
In the plaza,
In the fields.

I like to know
That mountains are there,
Around me,
So quiet,
So big
And so high.

I have heard
That clouds gather
In the mountains,
And that rainbows
Make bridges
Over them.

I have heard
That the Thunder sleeps
In the mountains,
With his great bow
And lightning arrows
By his side.

I have heard
That mountains
Are the home
Of the winds
And the night.

Perhaps
These things are true;
I have heard them.

Trees grow on mountains;
I have seen them
Growing.

I have seen great rocks
Hanging on mountains;
They do not want to fall.

Deer live in the mountains
And make little tracks
On the shores of lakes.

Baby rivers are there too.
And little white clouds
Look down on them
And want to play.

All things like mountains.
In summer
The rains stay there,

And only sometimes
Do they come down
To give water
To my Father's fields.

And snow
Would rather be on mountains
I think,
Because it is so slow
To go away from them.

The sun likes mountains too;
He paints them first
When he comes in the morning.
And at night
When the sun goes away
And hides from me,
He still looks back,
For I can see his colors
On the mountains.

Mountains
And animals
And plants,
We call them wild things.

Yet they help us in all ways.

We could not live
So well
If wild things
Did not help us.

The pueblo,
The people,
And fire,
And fields,
And water,
And land,
And animals—

I string them together
Like beads.

They make a chain,
A strong chain,
To hold me close
To home,
Where I live
In my Mother's house.